For new friends and true friends. —J.A.S.

To my parents, Jim & Jean, who let me be myself. —R.S.

First Green Light Readers edition 2017

www.hmhco.com
The text of this book is set in ITC Lubalin Graph Std.
The display type is set in ITC Lubalin Graph Std.

Library of Congress Cataloging-in-Publication Data is on file.

ISBN: 978-0-544-95949-1 paper over board
ISBN: 978-0-544-95902-6 paperback

Manufactured in China
SCP 10 9 8 7 6 5 4 3 2 1
4500661230

Woof & Quack in Winter

by Jamie A. Swenson

illustrated by Ryan Sias

Peachtree

Houghton Mifflin Harcourt
Boston   New York

I have fluffy down.
Not on your feet. You will have cold feet.
I will not have cold feet. I will stay with you.

So Quack did not fly south.
Snow started falling.

Snow covered everything.

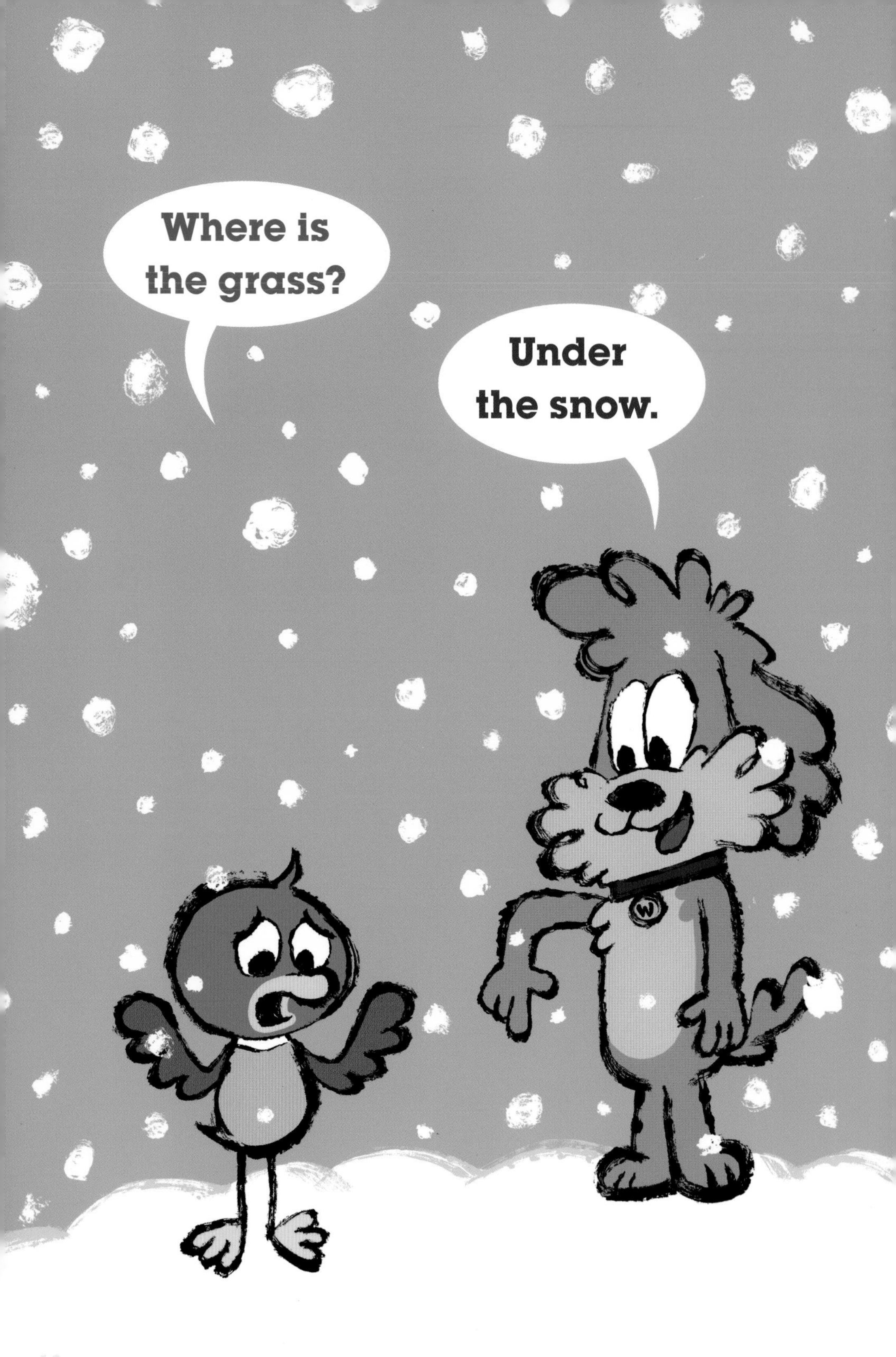
Where is the grass?
Under the snow.

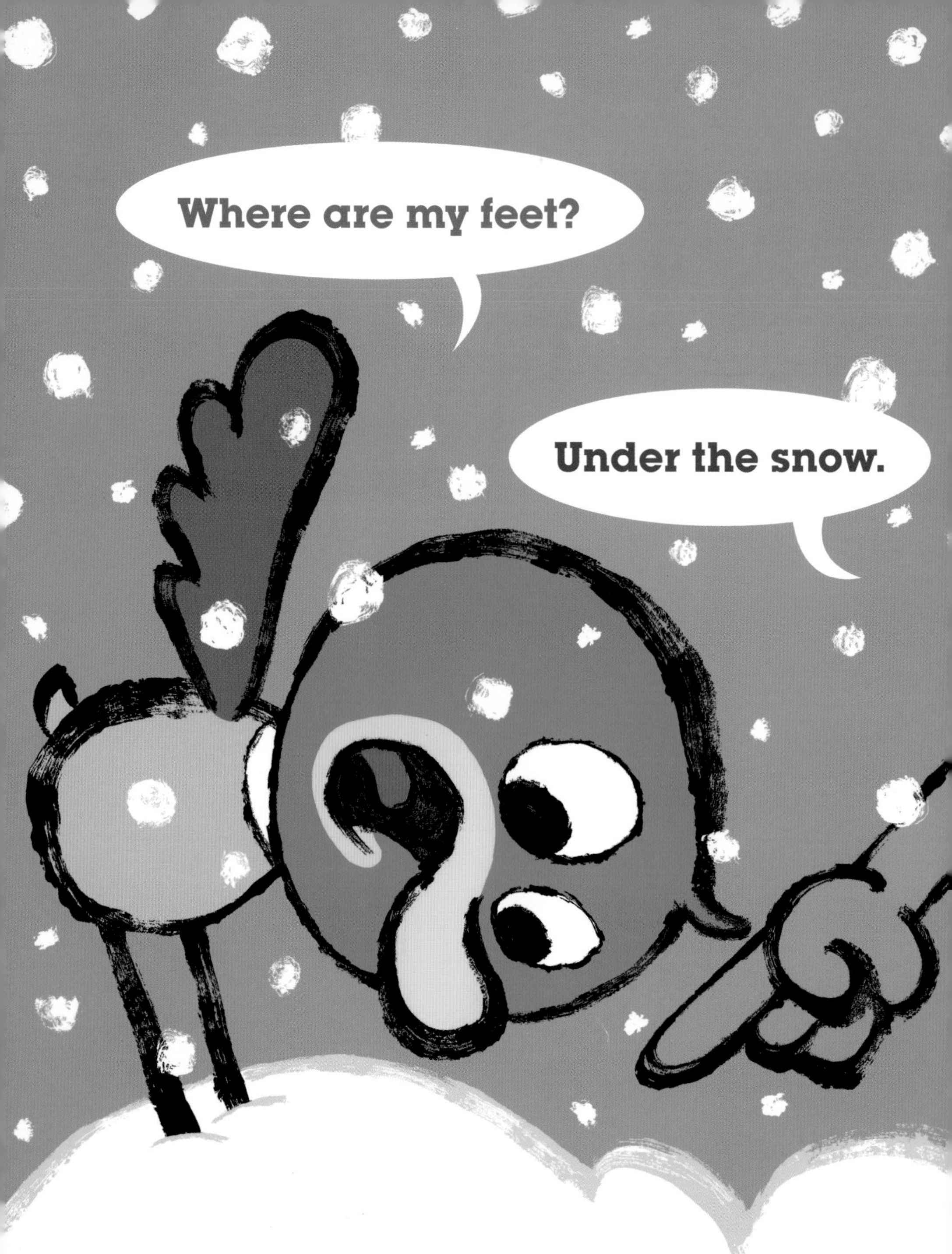
Where are my feet?
Under the snow.

13

Woof and Quack went sledding.

Woof and Quack made a snow duck.

Woof and Quack went ice skating.

BRRrrrrr!
Winter is fun. I am glad I stayed put.
I am glad you are here too. But this dog wants to fly south.
SHIVER
SHIVER

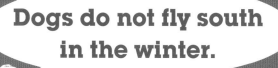

So Woof and Quack flew south.

Woof and Quack went sledding.

Woof and Quack made a sand dog.

Woof and Quack went swimming.